THE CONTEMPORARY
ART OF THE NOVELLA

THE CONTEMPORARY ART OF THE NOVELLA

SHOPLIFTING FROM AMERICAN APPAREL

SHOPLIFTING FROM AMERICAN APPAREL

TAO LIN

MELVILLEHOUSE
BROOKLYN, NEW YORK

SHOPLIFTING FROM AMERICAN APPAREL

© 2009 TAO LIN

MELVILLE HOUSE PUBLISHING
145 PLYMOUTH STREET
BROOKLYN, NY 11201

WWW.MHPBOOKS.COM

ISBN: 978-1-933633-78-7

FIRST MELVILLE HOUSE PRINTING: JULY 2009

BOOK DESIGN: KELLY BLAIR, BASED ON A SERIES DESIGN
BY DAVID KONOPKA

LIBRARY OF CONGRESS CATALOGING-IN-PUBLICATION DATA

LIN, TAO, 1983–
  SHOPLIFTING FROM AMERICAN APPAREL / TAO LIN.
    P. CM.
  ISBN 978-1-933633-78-7
  I. TITLE.
  PS3612.I517S56 2009
  813'.6—DC22

                                    2009012729

SHOPLIFTING FROM AMERICAN APPAREL

Sam woke around 3:30 p.m. and saw no emails from Sheila. He made a smoothie. He lay on his bed and stared at his computer screen. He showered and put on clothes and opened the Microsoft Word file of his poetry. He looked at his email. About an hour later it was dark outside. Sam ate cereal with soymilk. He put things on eBay then tried to guess the password to Sheila's email account, not thinking he would be successful, and not being successful. He did fifty jumping jacks. "God, I felt fucked lying on the bed," he said to Luis a few hours later on Gmail chat. "I wanted to fall asleep immediately but that is impossible. I need to fall asleep. Any second now. Just fall down asleep."

"I played video games," said Luis. "Perfect Dark. I killed people for two hours then I got bored. I know what you mean by impossible."

"This is fucked," said Sam.

"You know those people that get up every day, and do things," said Luis.

"I'm going to eat cereal even though I'm not hungry," said Sam.

"And are real proactive," said Luis. "And like are getting things done, and never quit their jobs. Those people suck."

"We get shit done too," said Sam. "Look at our books."

"I know, but that brings in no money," said Luis. "Are we, like, that word 'bohemians.' Or something. Our bios: 'They lived in poverty writing their masterpieces.'"

"We are the fucked generation," said Sam. "Someone release the press release announcing this. Look at that typo."

The word "announcing" was almost twice as long as normal.

"I'm laughing," said Luis. "That is a good typo."

"How do we get out of this," said Sam.

"'Their shoes were shit, they couldn't afford haircuts, they were stealing to stay alive, living off of strippers to create their art, but they believed that if they could write it something would happen,'" said Luis.

"Who are they," said Sam.

"They is us," said Luis.

"I'm alone," said Sam. "What would happen if I started sniffing coke."

"You would kill yourself in a panic attack."

"Are you sure," said Sam.

"You will be on coke trying to steal batteries and your mind won't be working properly and you will fuck up and someone will catch you and then you will go to jail."

"Oh yeah," said Sam. "I don't have to worry about money anymore, I just steal batteries."

"Do people really buy batteries off eBay," said Luis.

"Yes. I have undercut the competition. Walmart is crying."

"I'm going to watch cartoon porn," said Luis. "No I'm not. I'm going to look at Indian women. Have you ever fucked an Indian girl."

"No," said Sam. "Native American or Indian."

"You are awesome," said Luis. "Is her picture online."

"I'm confused," said Sam. "What are you talking about."

"How did you meet her," said Luis.

"No, I haven't," said Sam. "You're confused."

"What are you talking about," said Luis.

"I haven't had sex with one," said Sam.

"Okay," said Luis. "What are you talking about."

"Luis," said Sam. "What is happening. It's Saturday."

"I think we are going insane," said Luis. "From not being around people. We are starting to go inside ourselves, and play around inside of our own mental illness. That doesn't make any sense."

"What should I eat," said Sam. "I have two choices. Cereal or peanut butter bagel."

"Cereal," said Luis.

"I wanted the bagel. I'm eating the bagel, I don't know why I asked."

"Sheila didn't let you go over for leftovers," said Luis.

"No," said Sam. "I mean, we just didn't talk or something."

"Are you serious. Is everything okay."

"I don't know," said Sam. "I woke up at 3:30."

"I won't go to sleep until five in the morning," said Luis. "We are fucked."

"I woke at 10:30 then said 'this is fucked' and went back to sleep," said Sam. "I forced myself back to sleep."

"Sheila won't talk to you," said Luis. "Or is it because your cell phone broke."

"No," said Sam. "We just didn't talk since yesterday. We are like fighting or something. Or I just didn't email her or something."

"When Marissa and I fight we lay on our sides for an hour in different rooms and wait for the person that was mean to come into the room and say they are sorry, then we existentially attack each other in very quiet voices," said Luis.

"That sounds great," said Sam. "It's only 11 p.m. What are we going to do for six hours."

"Do you sometimes look up from the computer and look around the room and know you are alone, I mean really know it, then feel scared," said Luis.

"Yes," said Sam. "I really do that."

"Should we kill ourselves now or start crying or punch ourselves in the nuts," said Luis.

"What is wrong with us," said Sam. "Should I email Sheila. Or wait until she emails me. I have no car, phone, bike. I'm going to add more people on MySpace."

"We are so weird," said Luis. "We met online a year ago. And we are up a year later being weird as shit."

"One year," said Sam. "This is weird."

"I feel like my chest is going to explode," said Luis.

"I'm adding random people on MySpace," said Sam.

"I feel weird," said Luis. "Like I was molested by my uncle or something. You are on the floor. With the blanket around you."

"The blanket is over my head," said Sam.

"Are we fucked," said Luis and got off the internet.

Sam stared at his computer screen. He lay on his bed. It was November. Sam was in a rural area of Pennsylvania. He had moved here from New York City a few months ago to be near Sheila. He rolled off his bed and looked at his computer screen. Luis was back. "I just laid down and tried to cry," said Sam. "I made a noise."

"My computer took a shit for a second," said Luis.

"I can't think," said Sam. "I'm going to do push-ups. What if Sheila and I break up. I'd be so fucked."

"You still like each other right."

"Yeah," said Sam. "I don't know."

"I don't know what to do," said Luis. "Do you wake up most days and your first thoughts are of literature, you go to sleep thinking about literature."

"Yes," said Sam. "That is all I think about. If I'm having a shitty time with Sheila's mom I think about writing it in my novel later. I think about that the same time it's happening."

"When I'm talking to someone I think 'can I use this dialogue in a book,'" said Luis. "If the answer is no I try talking to someone else."

"Has Marissa ever threatened to kill you," said Sam.

"Oscar Wilde said that a genius is a spectator to their own life, to the point that the real genius is uninteresting," said Luis. "No, Marissa has never threatened to kill me."

"Oscar Wilde was stupid though," said Sam.

"Yeah, you're right," said Luis. "My chest is going to explode."

"My face is going to float away from my skull," said Sam. "To emo music."

"What are we going to do," said Luis. "We met each other in real life and didn't talk that much."

"I don't know," said Sam. "Publish more books."

Luis sent Sam a link to a porno site. "I already masturbated, should I really do it again," said Sam. "I already masturbated today also," said Luis. "If you need to I'll go away." "No, I'm just looking a little," said Sam. "Masturbation is an escape from literature," said Luis and emailed Sam a photo of a stripper.

"Is she sweating," said Sam.

"I think they oiled her down," said Luis.

"That's funny, I think," said Sam.

"We have been sitting here all night bullshitting and we still don't know what to do," said Luis.

"I'm going to masturbate then do some other shit then try to sleep for like 20 hours," said Sam. "Have a good night."

"Have a good night, I'm laughing," said Luis.

About four months later Sam was living with Sheila in a suburban area of Pennsylvania. He was alone in Sheila's mother's house drinking iced coffee and looking at his poetry on the computer screen. The room was sunny and Sam felt warm. He looked out the window at a compost pile and an aboveground swimming pool.

A few days later he and Sheila were on a train to New York City. They drank from a large plastic bottle containing organic soymilk, energy drink, and green tea extract and wrote sex stories to sell to nerve.com for $500. Sheila's sex story had chainsaws and Sam's sex story had Ha Jin doing things in a bathroom at Emory University. Sheila said she felt excited to be in New York City soon. They talked about making their own energy drink company. They got off the train and stood waiting for another train. They climbed a wall and sat in sunlight facing the train tracks.

"I feel really happy right now," said Sheila looking ahead.

Sam looked at the side of Sheila's face.

"You didn't feel happy before?" he said.

"I mean I just feel really good right now," said Sheila. "Don't you?"

"You don't feel good at other times?" said Sam staring at his new shoes. "I shouldn't have said that. Sorry. That was stupid of me."

"It's okay," said Sheila.

It was around 11 a.m. It was March.

Sam felt himself about to say something.

"Do you not feel good anymore?" he said.

Sheila had a bored facial expression.

"Something is wrong with me," said Sam.

They got off the wall and stood hugging each other. The train came and they got on and found a *New York Times Magazine* "Style Issue" and stood in an enclosed area between train cars with some other people. They pointed at things on each page and said "Which would you rather have?" or "Which would you rather be?" They pointed at a vacuum cleaner and a tree, a suitcase and a bottle of champagne, a small child and an old man. They chose the same thing each time. Sunlight came through trees passing by outside into the area where they stood. Sam noticed someone smiling at them and realized that for an amount of time he had not been aware of anything but what he and Sheila were doing.

Four months later Sam was living in his brother's studio apartment in Manhattan, sleeping on a mattress pad. He had not seen Sheila who now lived in Brooklyn in about two months. They emailed each other and then met one night at the Film Forum to see a documentary. In the lobby they didn't talk and Sam felt worried. He saw that Sheila had dressed nicely. In the movie a man said he was going to commit suicide but decided to walk instead and had now been walking for ten years. After the movie Sam said the man was probably walking to the gas station because his car broke. Sheila grinned and said "probably." They talked about a different movie and Sheila asked Sam if he wanted to see it together when it came out. Sam said he did. "What is that, look," he said about people standing on trash bags looking at each other.

"Freegans," said Sheila.

"There's so many," said Sam. "Why are there so many?"

"That's what they do," said Sheila.

"They look funny," said Sam. "They seem bored."

"I think one of them was Adam," said Sheila in a café. "He is like a famous freegan."

"I think I recognized Adam," said Sam. "Yeah, I saw him on *The View*, on YouTube. The people on *The View* made fun of him for being serious. It was funny. When they made fun of him for being serious he was still serious."

"He is very serious," said Sheila.

They stood talking near the front doors while looking at each other's shoes and other things. They left the café and went somewhere else then sat in front of New York University's business school. It was around 10 p.m. They ate most of a giant salad of hijiki, lettuce, spinach, sprouts, and tofu. Sam turned the aluminum container upside-down over a large plant. "High-quality fertilizer," he said.

"Good," said Sheila from where she sat. "Good job."

They talked about the salad's size and organic ingredients.

"We can eat it together in the future sometimes," said Sam.

"That would be good," said Sheila. "I would like that."

Sam pointed at a building across the street and said he used to live there. He remembered standing at a railing in a stairwell inside the building three or four years ago, in college on a

Friday night, listening to a self-help tape while thinking about killing himself. He remembered holding the tape player in his hand and looking at the earphone cord coming out of the tape player. The cord had seemed very strange.

"Are you going to the library now?" said Sheila.

"Yes," said Sam holding an iced coffee.

"Okay," said Sheila. "Thank you for the salad. Thank you for watching the movie with me."

"I am home and my internet is fixed," said Sheila in an email about an hour later. "I saw the freegans again. The Adam guy was eating a cupcake or something and he ate it really sloppy and walked around looking proud. I wanted to lecture him. I hope that you had a good night. Maybe we can hang out tomorrow." Sam emailed that he was going to a party with his publisher's intern tomorrow but that they could hang out a different day. After a few more emails Sam said he was going to work on things now. "Did you have a good night?" said Sheila. "You don't seem to respond a lot to my emails. I guess that's my fault but I'm just saying. Maybe you are emailing me more later." Sam emailed that he had a good night and felt bad about making Sheila feel bad. He asked if Sheila could go on Gmail chat.

"Hi," said Sheila on Gmail chat.

"Hi," said Sam. "I respond to other people's emails really short."

"Not everyone," said Sheila.

"Some people," said Sam.

"I'm trying to get myself to accept that you don't like me as much anymore and aren't interested in ever being with me again," said Sheila. "I feel really frustrated with myself."

"Were you angry I didn't write a long email back," said Sam.

"I wasn't angry just sad. I shouldn't be sad. I wish I wasn't sad."

"If we can just be nice with each other, and accepting, we can be friends."

"I know," said Sheila. "I feel so fucked."

"What if your friend kept telling you they felt fucked, and it was because you didn't like them as much as they liked you. That would make it so you would need to force yourself to like them more than you really do, just to get them to feel less fucked and happier. You would then want to get out of that situation. Because it's like being forced to do something you don't want to do."

"I know," said Sheila. "I'm sorry. I thought I could change that. You always told me I could change that. Now I don't understand. I feel a lot of sympathy for everyone. Out-of-control sympathy. An out-of-control amount of sympathy for everything."

"If you do that's good," said Sam with a worried facial expression.

"I will just do things until I am ready to accept that we will never get back together," said Sheila. "And when I have accepted that I will talk to you again."

A few weeks later Sam was walking to the library holding a large iced coffee. He had a reading in a few hours. He thought about the shirt he was wearing. He walked into American Apparel. He looked at things and sometimes touched things. He saw a person holding a book two inches from his face with his eyes over the top of the book. Sam thought the person was behaving strangely. A few minutes later Sam walked out of American Apparel holding an American Apparel shirt.

The person with the book made noises behind Sam on the sidewalk. "Do you work there?" said Sam. The person said he did. "Do you really work for American Apparel?" said Sam. The person displayed a police badge attached to his belt buckle beneath his oversized jersey. "Oh," said Sam.

They went inside. They went downstairs. Sam was photographed and put in handcuffs.

"Don't steal from us," said a manager looking at a computer screen. "Steal from some shitty corporation. We have fair-trade labor. I mean fair labor."

"I spend my money on even better places," said Sam. "Organic vegan restaurants."

"I'm all for that," said the manager.

Someone wrote "arrested" on Sam's photo and put it on the wall with about thirty other photos. The person who caught Sam put his head next to Sam's head and another photo was taken. "What are you trying to do, Luigi?" someone said. "Get a bonus?"

Two people behind Sam whispered things to each other.

A few seconds later someone took the handcuffs off Sam.

About fifteen minutes later two policemen arrived and put different handcuffs on Sam and walked him outside into a police car.

At the police station Sam was put in a cell with a bald Caucasian, a skinny Hispanic, and a tall Asian. Sam sat on a concrete bench. The tall Asian said he bought things from Duane Reade and went to Kmart and on the way out a security person stopped him and looked in his tote bag and saw shampoo and toothpaste from Duane

Reade and said he stole those things from Kmart and brought him into a room and told him to get into a cell. The tall Asian refused and the security person put him in a headlock and punched him and kicked him and emptied his tote bag and took his money.

The tall Asian made a motion of putting bills of cash into his chest pocket. Sam laughed then had a neutral facial expression. The tall Asian said Kmart was "running a racket." He said he didn't have money for a lawyer. He said he was an international student from Canada.

"Canada," said Sam.

A drunk man with blood inside his ears and on his face and shirt was put in the cell. Sam saw that the man looked like the Caucasian boxer in *Rocky V* that is trained by Rocky and then betrays Rocky. "I get punched in the face at Starbucks and I get thrown in jail?" screamed the drunk man. "You motherfuckers. I hope you motherfuckers are really enjoying your jobs. Fingerprinting people like me while fucking national security . . . matters of national security and fucking terrorists . . . this isn't fair. You motherfuckers." He sat on the bench. He stood and said "All right, I am the king of this cell. Everyone sit down. I am the king of this cell." He touched the skinny Hispanic.

"Hey man, don't touch me," said the skinny Hispanic. "I don't do nothing to you. I didn't do nothing to you, don't touch me." The drunk man looked at the skinny Hispanic. They shook hands. "Solidarity," thought Sam. "I'm covered in blood and I'm in jail," screamed the drunk man. "This isn't fair. I am going to ass-rape you so hard."

A policeman outside the cell said the drunk man would be ass-raped first and left the room.

"You don't want to fuck with a man who is smarter than Einstein," screamed the drunk man.

A policewoman told the drunk man to stop acting like an asshole.

"I get beat up in a bar and this is what I get," screamed the drunk man. "You motherpuggers, motherfuckers. I am so angry right now. I have so much respect for the armed forces. I respect you. You are the NYPD. That is awesome. With all due respect fuck you. You fuckers. Look at me. My shirt is covered in blood and I'm in jail." The drunk man walked into Sam sitting on the floor against a wall. The drunk man looked at Sam then screamed "Where is the other guy?" at a policeman outside the cell. "Is he here now? Just answer my question. Where is the other guy? Is he here?" The policeman said the other guy wasn't here. "Awesome," screamed the drunk man. "Awesome. Awesome. Awesome. Awesome. Awesome."

"What's your name?" said the tall Asian to the drunk man.

"Arthur," said the drunk man. "I took the intelligence test and I got a fucking 1520. 1580. I blew the lid off that test. Plus I'm big." The tall Asian asked the drunk man about being punched in Starbucks. "I got in a bar fight," said the drunk man. "I take some clients out and this is what I get." The tall Asian asked what happened to the other guy. "He ran away," said the drunk man.

It was quiet in the cell for a few minutes.

"I am going to kill everyone here," said the drunk man. "Is everyone okay with that? Is everyone in this cell okay with that? Let's get our word on that, okay? Raise your hand if you're okay with this." He touched the skinny Hispanic and the skinny Hispanic stood with an angry facial expression and said "Don't hit me. Don't hit me." The bald Caucasian stood in front of the drunk man with an angry facial expression. The police took the drunk man out of the cell. "You are never working in the union again," screamed the drunk man at the bald Caucasian.

"Union?" said the bald Caucasian laughing. "What the fuck are you talking about? I'm a drug dealer about to go away for a long time."

The police held the drunk man as he screamed obscenities.

"Where's your union now, bitch?" said the bald Caucasian.

The police put the drunk man in a different cell. "I get in a stupid bar fight and I'm covered in blood," he screamed out of view. "And I'm the one in jail. What about the other guy?"

"I thought you were in Starbucks," said a policeman.

"I was taking a shit in Starbucks, and I come out, and some guy hits me," said the drunk man. "I was in Starbucks," he screamed. "You don't believe me? I was in fucking McSorley's . . . the oldest bar . . . you motherfuckers. This isn't fair."

"Life isn't fair," said an African American policeman.

"You," screamed the drunk man loudly. "Life. You. You are bringing life into this? Don't do that you motherfucker. Don't fucking do that. You are bringing life into this. I can't believe you are doing this to me. I am so angry right now. I need to make some phone calls. I am running a failing business. I need to check my email." The drunk man called the African American policeman a nigger then said "You fat Irish boy who couldn't get a girlfriend so you became a cop, fuck you" to another policeman. The bald Caucasian shouted

"You rich whiny-ass white boy" and something about the drunk man's expensive watch. "My watch," screamed the drunk man. "Don't talk about my fucking watch you motherfucker. I am going to have sex with your little sister so hard. My watch. I have a fucking twenty-thousand-dollar Rolex you motherfucker. I don't wear it out. It's more expensive than . . . I am going to fucking sue all of you."

"That's what I'm talking about," said the bald Caucasian. "Rich white boy. That's what rich white boys do, they say they're going to sue you."

"Shut up," screamed the drunk man. "I'm trying to take a nap."

"When this first happened I was kind of angry," said the tall Asian. "Now I feel better. I don't know anyone this has happened to, you know, it's an experience."

A policeman took the bald Caucasian out to get his fingerprints on a machine outside the two cells. The skinny Hispanic stood and said he was in for possession of two ounces of marijuana. He said he had another bag of marijuana and pointed at his crotch and grinned. He touched his shoe and said there were pills inside. He said something about making $1,000 at Central Booking. The bald Caucasian came back and said the Fukanese ran Chinatown now. He said he sold

fireworks since he was eleven. He said every-
one used to eat well in Chinatown. Then the
Fukanese took over and fucked everything up.
He asked Sam what part of China he was from.
Sam said he was from Taiwan.

"You know that little island off China?" said
Sam.

"I know," said the bald Caucasian. "I am geo-
graphically sound."

A policeman said the drunk man had beaten
up a homeless person in Tompkins Square Park,
not gotten beat up at Starbucks. The drunk man
was snoring in the other cell. The bald Caucasian
and the skinny Hispanic talked about hurting
the drunk man. They discussed the placement
of surveillance cameras at Central Booking.
"He's drunk, people are different when they're
drunk," said the African American policeman in a
shy voice. "He might sober up and be the nicest
person you ever met."

The "fat Irish boy" policeman woke the
drunk man to get his fingerprints. It took about
ten minutes to get the drunk man's fingerprints.
The drunk man and the policeman hugged. The
tall Asian was released. The bald Caucasian went
in a side room with a policeman. "They told me
what I was getting," he said back in the cell. "I'm
going away for a long time." He talked about

killing the drunk man. A policeman gave Sam his belt and shoelaces. Sam signed a paper saying he would go to court. He walked to American Apparel. Luigi was on the sidewalk. Luigi grinned at Sam and went inside and got Sam's duffel bag.

"Thank you for shopping at American Apparel," said Luigi.

"You're welcome," said Sam. "Thank you for being nice to me. Good night."

At the library Sam emailed the organizer of the reading he was scheduled for that night, CC-ing the other reader. "I'm sorry I wasn't there today," said the email. "I was arrested earlier and got out around 9:30 in Manhattan somewhere. Was it okay without me? Very sorry about this."

The other reader replied asking if Sam wanted a free copy of his book.

Sam emailed the person his address and went outside. He bought an iced coffee and went back in the library.

"You seem strange," said Luis on Gmail chat a few hours later. "I'm pretty sure you have Asperger's. People with Asperger's and schizoid personality disorder usually make good friends."

"Schizoid," said Sam. "Luis. What are we."

"Fucked," said Luis. "Was that like a cheer. What are we! Fucked. Our shit can be studied by an anthropologist 1,000 years from now to know what we ate."

"Indian food," said Sam.

"They will say 'Sam had a vegan diet of good food and wine and Indian food. Luis ingested Waffle House.'"

"I want to change my novel to present tense," said Sam. "Is there some Microsoft Word thing to do that."

"I don't think so. I think you have to do it manually."

"Manually," said Sam.

"By hand," said Luis. "Get an interview on Suicide Girls, that should be your next step. Do you think in five years the national media will create a stupid term like 'blogniks' to describe us."

"Yes," said Sam. "Remember we had hope like 4 months ago."

"Can you cite that day," said Luis. "The day of hope."

"I remember one night particularly," said Sam. "Your book was at 30,000 sales rank. I was alone in the library. My fingers lay illuminated on the keyboard. Likewise my face was bathed in the soft blue light of Internet Explorer."

Sam stared at what he typed with a neutral facial expression.

"I just peed outside and hurt my foot," said Luis.

"You pee outside," said Sam. "Is it because of laziness. Or variety. I got arrested today, when I was stealing. I am okay. I just need to go to court on 9/11 and get community service."

"Just now," said Luis. "For what."

"Today around 4. A shirt. I was going to get a new shirt for my reading."

"Are you serious," said Luis. "9/11. Why didn't you tell me."

"I don't know. I wasn't thinking about it until you peed outside and I thought about variety." Sam emailed Luis around eight hundred words he had typed earlier about the holding cell. "The Asian guy got his ass beat for no reason and lost $100 and spent the day in jail," he said on Gmail chat.

"What did you do in there," said Luis.

"I sat there," said Sam.

"Were you scared. What did you do."

"We sat there," said Sam. "I felt the same sort of."

"What did your brain do," said Luis.

"I was trying not to laugh at the drunk guy. The Asian guy was like in Kafka. He didn't steal anything and got his ass beat and will probably be deported to Canada."

"Who beat his ass," said Luis.

"Kmart. I think they chose him because he looks like he doesn't care if he gets his ass beat for no reason. I think Kmart saw that in him."

"Kmart beat his ass," said Luis. "Are you worried. Have you told your parents."

"I'm not telling them," said Sam. "Unless they ask."

Sam talked about his parents having moved to Taiwan.

"Your parents have returned to their native land to die?" said Luis. "Are they like living there now, like that is their life?"

"Yes," said Sam. "I think."

"Are you okay, my friend," said Luis.

"I don't know," said Sam. "Are you."

"I haven't been arrested and my parents haven't left the country I'm residing in. I don't speak to my parents but I'm already over that. So it is different with you. You didn't tell me that. I feel like petting your head."

"My mom emails me," said Sam. "I am okay."

"Don't steal shit for a while," said Luis. "And try to make yourself happy in some way."

"Okay," said Sam. "I'll buy a new emo CD."

"Do you have a lawyer," said Luis. "Do you

have connections. When I went to court I told them I was a Hersado and the charges were dropped magically. My grandfather owns a grocery store in Youngstown."

"I have no lawyer," said Sam. "I might get a job."

"You have good rankings on Amazon," said Luis. "Soon you will be making money to write and be weird, and not have to steal."

Sam said he was going to eat Chinese food.

"Go eat," said Luis. "It is a beautiful night."

In court Sam saw the tall Asian sitting with a person who looked like an attorney. The tall Asian looked at the person, the person said something, and the tall Asian walked out of the courtroom. Sam's attorney said Sam's record would be erased after six months if he chose two days' community service instead of one. Sam had borrowed $1,000 from his brother to hire an attorney. About fifteen people received community service for possessing marijuana or shoplifting and then Sam's name was called. Sam and his attorney stood in front of the judge. Sam's attorney said something about two days' community service. The judge looked at Sam and read the same statement she read to everyone else. Sam went upstairs and scheduled his community service.

A few weeks later Sam went to Tompkins Square Park around 8 a.m. and changed trash bags with a large group of people. Someone said one bag was "heavy as bricks" and the bag broke and two bricks fell out. One bag in the dog run was very heavy with dog shit and would not leave the trashcan. Someone said "Fuck that bag" and the bag wasn't changed. The second day a person on his third of five days of community service said he robbed a car last night and left his cell phone inside the car. The person asked Sam and two other people if he would be okay. Sam said the person would be okay because his name wasn't in the cell phone. The person said his name was written on the cell phone. Sam walked around with a grabbing stick and grabbed many Colt 45s. On his break he bought a strawberry-banana-soymilk smoothie and drank it walking back to the park.

Around 3 p.m. Sam was standing inside an enclosed area on the edge of the park holding a trash bag and the grabbing stick, staring into the distance, when he saw Travis, a manager at the organic vegan restaurant where he now worked, looking at him.

"I didn't know you volunteered," said Travis.

"I have two days' community service," said Sam.

"Oh, I had this once," said Travis grinning.

Sam moved the grabbing stick around in the air. He had been moving slowly to prevent himself from sweating. It was early October and a little warm.

At work Sam put two scoops of brown rice into a "small Chinese container." He walked past Julia and opened a small metal door. He scooped steamed vegetables into the container. Julia carried a tray of potatoes out of the kitchen. Ben looked at Sam and said something.

"What," said Sam.

Ben repeated what he had said.

"What," said Sam.

"Did you tell Julia we need more beans?" said Ben.

Sam thought about saying "what" many more times

"Oh," he said in voice louder than normal. "No."

Ben walked past Sam to Julia.

"Julia, we really need beans," said Ben.

"Okay," said Julia. "Beans."

Julia walked to the beans and moved the ladle around. She stared at the dining room for a few seconds. She walked to the back of the kitchen, leaned against a counter, and looked at Sam with a neutral facial expression. Sam felt that his face displayed no reaction. He walked to a central area of the kitchen and stood with unfocused eyes. Ben was thirty-nine, Sam knew from Facebook. Sam had a poem in the "drafts" section of his Gmail account called "ben is funny at work." Sam felt himself grinning. He stopped grinning and stared at different things while people around him worked. "I feel tired of life," he said out loud. "I don't feel like working anymore."

"What was that?" said Ben.

"What," said Sam.

"What did you say, you're tired?" said Ben.

"I'm tired of life. I don't want to do any more work. But I still want to be paid."

Ben laughed with a serious facial expression. "Just don't slit your wrists on the cutting board," he said. "It'll stain the wood."

"I would go downstairs to commit suicide," said Sam. "I'll hang myself in the bathroom. José-Manuel will find me."

"Good," said Ben. "Maybe he'll finally learn to knock."

"Really?" said Sam. "He doesn't knock?"

"No, he does," said Ben. "I'm joking."

"Oh," said Sam.

"Do you mind if I go downstairs for a bit," said Ben later. "I'm going to use the bathroom."

"No," said Sam. "Go ahead."

A few minutes later Julia came upstairs with two trays of tempeh. "Ben was standing there," she said. "I asked him what he was doing. He said he was waiting for you to do some tickets." Julia grinned and stared at Sam like she was about to make her eyebrows go up and down.

"That's funny," said Sam. "Ben is passive-aggressive."

"I know you usually do the most work," said Julia.

"I'm not even 'phone person' tonight," said Sam. "Ben is confused."

On Christmas Eve Sam woke around 7 p.m. in his brother's studio apartment in Manhattan. Sam had moved in November into a four-person apartment in Brooklyn but was staying at his brother's studio apartment while his brother was on vacation with his girlfriend. Sam put on music very loud and showered in the dark with the bathroom door open. He put in earphones and walked ten blocks to an organic raw vegan restaurant. He ate a seaweed salad. He drank a smoothie. He walked back to the apartment. He drank an energy drink. He worked on writing for two and a half hours. He lay on his brother's queen-size bed listening to music. He read most of the newest Stephen Dixon novel and fell asleep around 3 a.m.

On New Year's Eve Sam lay on his mattress in Brooklyn reading short stories. He heard fireworks outside. He stood on his mattress and stared out his window at a deli.

Around 11:30 p.m. he got a text message from Kaitlyn: "2008 drunk by 8."

After midnight he got a text message from Mallory: "2008 feels insane."

Sam grinned and text messaged: "It does. Feels like 2040 or something." He showered and dried himself. He lay on his mattress and thought about writing a novel about working hard and becoming rich and living alone in a giant house in Florida. Loneliness and depression would be defeated with a king-size bed, an expensive stereo system, a drum set, a bike, an unlimited supply of organic produce and coconuts, and maybe calmly playing an online role-playing game. Each day the person in the novel would lay in sunlight on the living room carpet listening to music in "surround-sound" while drinking iced coffee. At night the person would ride a bike around the neighborhood or drink smoothies while taking very long baths.

A few days later Sam met Kaitlyn in Williamsburg to go to the annual work party for the organic vegan restaurant where he worked. Kaitlyn had a "Synergy" brand kombucha in her jacket pocket. She said she dropped it earlier and it made a very loud noise and people looked at her. "Drop it now," said Sam. "No," said Kaitlyn. Sam tried to take the kombucha and it went further into Kaitlyn's jacket pocket. "I can't get it, why is it sliding away," said Sam. "Stop trying to grab my kombucha," said Kaitlyn laughing. A few minutes later Sam gained control of Kaitlyn's kombucha and dropped it and it made a very loud noise.

The work party was at a taco restaurant with a bar. Keith looked at Sam and Kaitlyn and gave Sam four drink tickets. Sam and Kaitlyn put food on plates and sat at the bar and ordered mojitos. Kaitlyn drank hers quickly. Sam drank his slowly.

There was a Magic 8-Ball on the bar.

"Is Kaitlyn going to get drunk tonight?" said Sam.

The 8-Ball said "doubtful."

"Is Sam going to get drunk tonight?" said Kaitlyn.

The 8-Ball said "doubtful."

"Is the owner going to get drunk?" said Sam.

The 8-Ball said "chances are good" the owner of the organic vegan restaurant Sam worked at would get drunk. The owner was in her fifties. Sam said the owner wasn't a vegan because her doctor had told her to eat meat. Sam saw the owner walking alone about thirty feet away, taller than everyone else. "I got really drunk last week when I was home in Michigan," said Kaitlyn. "I went into a park to go to sleep but then I got up and walked ten blocks to a hospital."

"What," said Sam quietly while grinning.

"Is corn in the same food group as grains?" he said.

"Probably," said Kaitlyn.

"Tell the DJ to play rap," said Sam.

Kaitlyn went and told the DJ to play Lil Wayne.

"He said 'no,'" said Kaitlyn grinning at Sam.

They left the bar and sat on a sofa facing the bar. "Do you think those two girls standing by that guy are going to make out?" said Kaitlyn.

"That's a man," said Sam.

Kaitlyn took out stationery she bought earlier that day. Sam waved at Paula who was talking to Matt. "Do you want stationery?" said Kaitlyn a few minutes later to Paula. "I want stationery," said Sam. Briana walked by and knocked over Sam's mojito which was on the floor. Briana walked away. "Did people get really drunk last year?" said Sam.

"Ben got really drunk and fell down," said Paula.

"That's funny," said Sam. "I wish he would fall down now."

Paula looked at Sam with a concerned facial expression.

"Ben is in Brazil right now," said Sam slowly.

"That's right, Ben is in Brazil, so he isn't here," said Paula.

"That's funny," said Sam. "Ben fell down."

Paula walked away. Sam took Kaitlyn's hat and put it over his face. "Stop, you're stretching it," said Kaitlyn. They went to the bar and Kaitlyn ordered a Jack and Coke and Sam ordered another mojito. They went to the front of the restaurant and looked at everyone. Paula was at a table with tarot cards opposite Laura and Laura's boyfriend. Let's go back to the sofa," said Kaitlyn. "It's the best spot." They went to the sofa then went to the bar. Sam introduced Kaitlyn to Matt. Sam looked at Kaitlyn's face as she talked to Matt. Keith gave Sam and Kaitlyn two more drink tickets. Matt walked away. José-Manuel came out of a bathroom and looked at Kaitlyn then stared at Sam. "José-Manuel," said Sam. "Sam," said José-Manuel and patted Sam's shoulder and walked away. Kaitlyn ordered a mystery drink. "Mystery drink?" said the bartender.

"Is the bartender drunk?" said Kaitlyn.

The 8-Ball said "chances are good."

"Look at the owner," said Sam. "She is dancing alone, lost in her drunkenness."

Kaitlyn laughed and said "That's sad."

"I think she's just confused," said Sam.

They left the bar and sat on the sofa. Sam took Kaitlyn's mystery drink and put some in his mojito and some fell on the sofa. The mystery drink was red. The man Kaitlyn thought was a girl looked at the sofa and said something. Sam made a guilty facial expression at Kaitlyn.

They walked to where Paula was sitting with her tarot cards.

"Am I next," said Sam staring at the table.

"You're next," said Paula.

"What is it," said Sam with Paula, Kaitlyn, Laura, and Laura's boyfriend looking at him. "Should I," he said with unfocused eyes. "Do it, get your reading," said Kaitlyn. Laura and her boyfriend walked away. Kaitlyn and Sam sat. Paula moved the tarot cards around and said things.

Kaitlyn was staring toward Paula but not at Paula.

"Are you asleep?" said Sam.

Kaitlyn said she wasn't asleep just drunk.

"What," said Paula in a nervous voice.

"Sam asked if I was asleep," said Kaitlyn. "I'm just drunk."

Paula said the tarot cards said Sam would be rich if he sold out. "It said 'sold out'?" said Sam. "Yes," said Paula with a serious facial expression. "That's funny," said Sam. Someone said the restaurant was closing. Amy hugged Paula from behind and said everyone was going to a bar across the street.

"It's just a door," said Amy. "You'll find it."

"Where, though?" someone said. "I mean, I don't know."

"We can find it," said Sam. "We'll just look for it."

Outside the taco restaurant a man was telling a policeman in a police car that someone around the block was 6′ 4″ and white and drunk. Paula said she didn't know anyone that tall. Sam said it was Henry. Sam ran to the corner and ran back and said "It's Henry." "Really?" said Paula. "No, it's not Henry," said Sam. They walked toward the bar. Sam picked up a very long stick and said he was going to stir his drink with it. He hit Kaitlyn's head with the stick. She broke the stick and ran away. "Stop running," shouted Sam.

At the bar they sat at a table and Kaitlyn put her arm around Sam's waist.

"I like Rufus Wainwright, is that okay?" she said.

"What movie was he in," said Sam.

"He's a singer," said Kaitlyn.

"Oh, is he really old?" said Sam.

"No," said Kaitlyn. "That's his dad."

Paula and Matt were sitting opposite Sam and Kaitlyn. Sam called Paula's cell phone with his cell phone. Paula answered and Sam hung up. Kaitlyn asked if Sam wanted a drink.

"Do you want to share one?" said Sam.

"Yes," said Kaitlyn and left the table and came back with two glasses of vodka and grapefruit juice. "Did they give you one for free?" said Sam. Kaitlyn laughed and said "no." Sam put out the flame in the candle. Kaitlyn got a lighter from people at another table and lit the candle.

Later Travis was hugging Enrique near the bar and they stumbled for about ten feet and fell down, knocking over a bench. Amy and Yvonne were kissing by the bar. Alex sat by Kaitlyn and looked at Sam. "It's funny to see you in this environment, in a bar," he said loudly to Sam. "I mean usually you're so reserved at work. So it's funny to see you here, in a bar." Juan sat across from Kaitlyn with a very serious facial expression and talked about burns on his face from hot oil at work.

Briana was taking photos of everyone using flash.

"Are you taking photos for something?" said Sam.

Someone said Briana was taking photos for herself.

Sam saw that Juan was laughing very loudly.

Kaitlyn was talking into her cell phone.

"Are you taking photos for something?" said Sam.

"Yeah," said Briana. "I'm taking photographs for *New York Magazine* about famous writers getting drunk," she said. "MySpace. Facebook."

"Flickr," said Sam.

"No," said Briana.

"Photobucket," said Sam.

"Yes," said Briana. "Photobucket."

Sam took Kaitlyn's cell phone and text messaged Kaitlyn's sister: "I'm really drunk. I'm in trouble." Kaitlyn took her phone back laughing and resent the text message by accident. "Fuck," she said and pressed buttons and resent the text message again by accident while laughing. She called her sister and left a voicemail saying she wasn't in trouble while Sam shouted "drunk" toward the phone.

"Doesn't it smell strange if you burn hair?" said Sam.

"Take some of my hair," said Kaitlyn.

Sam took some of Kaitlyn's hair and put it in the candle.

"It smells like a corpse," said Sam.

"It smells like cereal," said Kaitlyn.

The candle went out and someone said "no."

"I'm with Sam in a bar," said Kaitlyn into her phone. "I'm talking to Joseph," she said to Sam. "He says you're his favorite living writer. He said he found your book on the toilet in the house he's living in or something and read it and liked it. Then he walked around and found another one of your books on a picnic table and read it and liked it."

"That's funny," said Sam. "Toilet. Picnic table."

Kaitlyn finished talking to Joseph and called someone else.

"People hate you when you call them late at night drunk," said Sam.

"No they don't," said Kaitlyn very loudly. "I'm going to call whoever I want."

Sam looked at a text message from Paula: "I'm

not good at drinking. Play Scrabble soon with me?" "Why the fuck are you guys open twenty-four hours now?" said Kaitlyn into her cell phone. Sam text messaged Paula: "We should watch the Scrabble movie and play Scrabble at the same time."

Kaitlyn and Sam went upstairs into an outdoor area and each did a cartwheel. Kaitlyn broke a glass and covered her mouth with her hand. Sam covered his mouth with his hand then tried to climb onto the roof.

"You can't climb that," someone said. "And this area is closing."

Outside the bar Kaitlyn said something about the J train. "Unless you want to let me sleep on your sofa," she said. They got on the L train and arrived at Sam's apartment. Sam asked Kaitlyn if she wanted to see his new computer. They went in his room and sat on the floor with their legs on each other's legs. Sam stood and looked down at Kaitlyn. "You'll be cold without a blanket on the sofa," he said.

"That's okay," said Kaitlyn looking ahead. "Unless you want me to sleep in here. It's up to you."

"You can sleep in here," said Sam.

"Okay," said Kaitlyn.

"I'm going to use the bathroom," said Sam. "Do you want to use the bathroom?" Kaitlyn shook her head no. Sam washed his face and peed and went in his room. Kaitlyn was sitting on the mattress staring at the floor. "What are you doing?" said Sam laughing. Kaitlyn grinned and said she was drunk and laid down on the mattress. Sam jumped on the mattress. He sat on the mattress. He lay on the mattress. He took stuffed animals and put them around him and Kaitlyn. He said his ex-girlfriend Sheila made them.

"What's this one?" said Kaitlyn.

Sam said it was a hamster.

"No it isn't, what's this," said Kaitlyn holding things which came out of the hamster's head. Sam said "antlers" and threw the stuffed animals at the ceiling and they fell on him and Kaitlyn. Sam asked Kaitlyn to turn off the light. Kaitlyn turned off the light. Sam held an Eeyore stuffed animal above him and said Eeyore's problem was that his tail fell off.

"That's sad," said Kaitlyn. "It's not true."

"What?" said Sam grinning.

"Do you snore?" he said.

"I don't snore," said Kaitlyn.

"What if I snore?" said Sam.

Kaitlyn said she would elbow him.

"What if I say 'Eeyore, Eeyore' when I'm asleep?" said Sam.

Kaitlyn said she would elbow him a lot. "Eeyore smells like coconut oil," she said. "Everything here smells like coconut oil," said Sam. "I rub it on myself then roll around in bed." He put his arm under the back of Kaitlyn's neck and she turned toward him putting her arm across his chest. They lay quietly without moving. Some light came in the window.

"I saw Sheila on the street today," said Sam. "It was really awkward. She was with her friend and she came toward me and I thought she was going to stop to talk to me but then only her friend stood in front of me and she was walking away and her friend said 'hi, I'm Gerard.' I said 'hi, I'm Sam.' Then I said 'good night' and went in the subway."

"Gerard," said Kaitlyn. "Was it her new boyfriend?"

"I don't think so," said Sam. "No, just a friend, I think. Yeah, just a friend."

"Do you still like her?"

"I don't know," said Sam.

"But you still love the things she made you, right?"

"Yeah," said Sam.

"Then why don't you like her anymore?"

"I don't know," said Sam. "I do like her."

They were quiet for about a minute.

"Why was she mean to you today?" said Kaitlyn in a confused voice.

"I don't know," said Sam. "She wasn't."

They were quiet for a few minutes.

"I'm going to sleep now," said Kaitlyn.

"Okay," said Sam and rolled over facing a wall. "Good night."

"Good night," said Kaitlyn.

The next week Paula and Sam played Scrabble in her apartment then watched a Scrabble documentary on her computer. A Scrabble player had sex with a prostitute in Mexico during a tournament in San Diego. Paula and Sam went to her room and sat on her bed. They kissed and Paula began to move around a lot. Paula was scratching Sam's back. Sam thought "voracious" and felt confused. Paula crawled on the bed and gave Sam a condom and Sam put it on.

"I don't like condoms," he said kneeling on the bed.

"What should I do?" said Paula. "What do you want me to do?"

"Nothing. It's okay."

"I'm sorry," said Paula.

"Don't worry," said Sam.

"Okay," said Paula.

They went to sleep and woke around 8 a.m. and ate leftover bread from the organic vegan restaurant where they worked. Paula put kimchee and vegan mayonnaise on her bread. Sam had read about her doing that on her blog. Sam asked if he could put Paula's agave nectar on his bread. Paula said he could. Sam ate two pieces of bread. At her front door they hugged and Sam thought about one night at work when Paula stared at a wall at the back of the kitchen while eating rice pudding. Sam had walked to her and asked what she was doing. She had turned around with a shy facial expression and Sam had grinned at her for a few seconds. Sam liked shy facial expressions. "I feel good hugging Paula," he thought.

On Hester's sofa in her apartment in Chelsea Sam said he had sort of been seeing someone named Paula for a few weeks but didn't think they would see each other anymore. Hester asked why and Sam said he didn't know. Hester asked again and Sam said he didn't know. Hester said she needed to pee and went to the bathroom and came back and sat on Sam's lap and began to kiss him. Sam tasted mouthwash.

Hester stood and walked around and said she shouldn't be doing that. She said Sam was too young. She sat on Sam's lap and they kissed and she stood and walked around.

"I'm one year younger than you," said Sam. "You aren't making sense."

"I'm not going to have sex with you," said Hester standing near her front door, almost out of view. "Should we go buy cigarettes and condoms?" she said not looking at Sam. "I'm out of cigarettes. I haven't had sex in so long."

"I don't know," said Sam after a few seconds.

"Why don't you want to have sex with me?" said Hester.

"What do you mean," said Sam.

"I don't know," said Hester quickly.

"I don't . . . not don't want to have sex with you," said Sam.

About a week later they were on Hester's sofa watching child prodigies on YouTube. They watched a video called "don't hate me because i'm a child prodigy." They began to drink wine. They lay stomach-down on her bed. Hester said she was engaged to a poet in Kansas when she was twenty and then ran away and the poet cried in a basement. Sam asked questions about the poet and Hester talked for about an hour. Sam felt very emotional thinking about the poet. Hester asked Sam if he wanted to go to an event where Moby was DJ-ing.

"Yes," said Sam. "Will you hang out with Moby?"

"I usually sit in a room downstairs talking to Brandon," said Hester.

"That sounds good. I'll just sit by you and look at things."

"Brandon is friends with Moby or something," said Hester. "They talk on AIM like every day. Brandon is great. I love him. He can get really jealous though." Hester said one time Brandon saw her kissing someone and then went upstairs and threw a chair and broke a table and banned her from a lot of New York City clubs for a few months. "I've told him I'm not interested in him like that, and I've never even kissed him or anything," said Hester. "So he really doesn't have any reason to act like that. I don't understand."

"He just likes you a lot," said Sam. "I'm afraid."

The next week Sam went to Hester's apartment at night and lay on her sofa. He said he went to an organic vegan muffin store earlier with Robert. He said he liked Robert. "I should probably get dressed," said Hester and walked away and walked back wearing tights under her dress. She stared at edamame that Sam was eating from a bowl. They went outside and got in a cab. At the club they walked to the front of the line and a person let them in. "Who was that, did you know them," said Sam. "No," said Hester. "Oh, good," said Sam. They got drinks and walked into a garage area with Brandon. Sam said it smelled like fish in the garage. Sam drank all of his vodka and grapefruit juice. "Sam, you drank that really fast," said Hester. "It didn't seem to have any alcohol in it," said Sam and stared at things while Brandon and Hester talked to each other.

"What is your opinion on string theory, is it real," said Sam to Brandon.

"It's fake," said Brandon. "There's one that's real. I can't remember what it's called." He looked toward the ceiling without moving his head or neck.

About ten seconds passed.

"I read *Chaos* by James something," said Sam.

Hester laughed. Sam felt her looking at him.

"Yes, chaos theory," said Brandon. "James Gleick."

Brandon walked out of the garage area.

"Do you like skateboarders?" said Sam to Hester.

Hester made some noises.

"I like skateboarders," said Sam. "I watch the skating things on Vice TV."

Two Asian men came into the garage area and began to smoke.

"Do they work in the restaurant," said Sam.

"I don't know, probably," said Hester. "Do you skateboard?"

"In middle school." Sam stared at Hester's face.

Hester said something about Brandon eating pike at 4 a.m.

"That's good," said Sam staring at Hester's face. "I watch skateboarders on YouTube. I feel like we're in Taiwan right now. I think because of the fish smell, it reminds me of restaurants in Taiwan. Restaurants in Taiwan are all, like, really big, and have giant tables with those spinning things in the middle, and TVs." Sam thought about talking about the twenty-four-hour mall in Taiwan. The twenty-four-hour mall was funny. Sam wondered if he was talking too much. He thought that he usually didn't talk so it would be okay if he talked a lot while he was feeling calm and alert.

"I feel good," he said with some confidence.

Brandon came back and said the name of the string theory he believed was correct. The name was a combination of letters and numbers.

Brandon walked away. Sam and Hester went downstairs into a room and sat on a padded seat. People came out of a door and smiled at Sam and Hester. Sam smiled at them and waved and they went upstairs.

"Are you bored," said Hester.

"No, I feel calm," said Sam. "I like Brandon."

They went upstairs and stood in a crowded hallway. Sam stared at people's faces with a neutral facial expression. Someone was taking pictures of everyone with a professional-looking camera. Brandon said something and walked away. "Go," said Hester. "He wants to introduce you to Moby."

"Go with Brandon," said Hester.

"Who," said Sam. "Oh, he was talking to me?"

"Yes," said Hester.

Sam went downstairs and stood by Brandon. Moby was standing with some people.

"He's talking to girls right now," said Brandon.

"I don't have to meet him," said Sam.

"He's weird sometimes," said Brandon with a serious facial expression. Brandon and Sam sat on a padded seat. Moby walked by and Brandon stood and said Sam's name.

"Hi, we met before," said Sam from where he sat.

Moby looked at Sam and quietly said "hi" and walked away.

"He's weird," said Brandon in a voice like he was going to cry.

"It's okay," said Sam. "Hester said you play violin."

Brandon nodded a little. "I'm sorry about that," he said. "I'll introduce you at a different time, maybe. It'll be better later. He's nervous now."

"It's okay," said Sam. "Hester said you like computers. I play piano."

"Oh, really," said Brandon with a confused facial expression.

"Yeah. I like Chopin. I feel like Chopin is 'emo.' Do you like Chopin?"

"Schumann . . . is my favorite," said Brandon.

"When you DJ," said Sam. "Do you use, like, polyrhythms."

"Um, sometimes," said Brandon in a quiet voice.

Sam said he was going to find Hester and walked away.

About a month later Sam was walking toward the library around 4 p.m. after taking the L train to Manhattan and buying food. He text messaged Robert: "Not going to Mara's party. Holding iced coffee, feel potentially very productive. Staying in library tonight." He walked into New York University's computer store. He picked up Sony "in-ear" earphones and walked around and removed the security tag. He put the earphones in his pocket. He walked toward the exit. "What do you have in your pocket?" said a short Hispanic woman with short hair. Sam stared at the woman and remembered seeing her standing in a corner sort of looking at him about forty seconds ago.

Sam took out his cell phone. "My cell phone."

"You have something else," said the woman.

"I have this," said Sam holding the earphones.

"Where did you get those?" said the woman.

"They're mine, I brought them in."

"You didn't bring those in. I saw you take them."

"No, they're mine," said Sam.

"Let me see them," said the woman.

"You caught me," said Sam grinning. "They're from this store."

"Okay, just stand here," said the woman. "Don't move."

Sam thought about running away. His iced coffee would spill a lot. The woman was saying things into a walkie-talkie. A middle-aged man came and walked Sam next door into New York University's security center.

"Are you a student?" said the middle-aged man.

"Yes, no," said Sam. "I'm an alumni."

"He had twenty-eight dollars in his pocket," said the middle-aged man to another middle-aged man. "How much were the earphones?" he said to Sam.

"I don't know," said Sam. "I think forty."

"This is your first time being arrested?"

"Yes," said Sam in an uncertain voice.

The middle-aged man put Sam's full iced coffee in a trashcan. The middle-aged man put Sam in handcuffs. Two policemen came about twenty minutes later and asked Sam if he had been arrested before. "Yes," said Sam slowly. "I mean, I don't know if I have a record. I had a D.A.T. and I think it was erased from my record after six months, I don't know if it's been six months."

"You told me you didn't have a prior arrest," said the middle-aged man.

"Sorry," said Sam. "I mean, I didn't know."

"What were you arrested for the first time?" said the middle-aged man.

"Shoplifting," said Sam.

"From the same store?" said the middle-aged man.

"No," said Sam. "From American Apparel."

"Are you going to shoplift again?" said the middle-aged man. "The answer is no."

"No," said Sam. "I shouldn't have today. I'm just stupid."

At the police station Sam called Robert. "Hi," he said to Robert's voicemail. "I'm at the police station on Fifth Street, can you come get my bag? If you don't come that's okay. If you come you can eat the grapes in the bag. They're organic." Sam did sit-ups on the concrete bench in the cell. The bench was very smooth. Sam did push-ups with his hands on the bench and his feet on the floor. He thought that he would have a headache soon from no caffeine. He looked at a teenage girl in handcuffs on a bench outside the cell. "What are you here for?" said the girl.

"Stealing earphones," said Sam.

"Why did you steal earphones?"

"Mine broke," said Sam.

"Earphones are 4.99," said the girl.

"No, but I wanted forty-dollar ones," said Sam.

The girl said she stole from Urban Outfitters. "I was outside, and the guy told us to stop, and I thought about running. I thought there was a sixty percent chance I would get away if I ran and

I decided not to run. I wasn't even the one that stole the most. My friend was holding the bag with everything in it, she ran and got away."

"She got away," said Sam. "That's funny."

"Yeah, she just started running. She ran into the subway."

A policeman asked if Sam wanted anything from the vending machine. Sam asked if he could have food from his bag. The food was organic raw vegan "Raweos." The policeman asked what the food was.

"Like, cookie things," said Sam. "Cookies."

"No, I think we better not do that," said the policeman.

Four people Sam's age were put in the cell. They sat without talking. The teenage girl began asking them questions. They were college students from Boston who had been caught smoking marijuana on their hotel balcony.

"Are you seeing Michelle after this?" said the policeman in the driver's seat on the way to Central Booking. "I think I'm meeting her and her friends at that bar we were at last night," said the other policeman. "Are you going right after this?" said the policeman in the driver's seat. "Yeah, probably I'll just head over straight after this," said the other policeman. "Change at the station. Try to get this wrapped up in an hour. I like Michelle." In Chinatown the police got out of the car. The teenage girl and Sam were in the backseat in handcuffs. The teenage girl said something about "the hot officer."

"Which one," said Sam.

The teenage girl said the one that was driving.

"Would you go out with him," said Sam.

"Hell no," said the teenage girl.

"Why not," said Sam.

"I don't know," said the teenage girl.

They got out of the car and went in a building. Sam remembered having walked past the building maybe two hundred times when he lived nearby a few years ago. Sam stood in line and went downstairs. Someone took Sam's photo with very bright flash. Sam went further downstairs. Sam was given a peanut butter sandwich and put into a cell with a toilet, a payphone, and about ten people.

"What are you in for?" someone said.

"Shoplifting," said Sam grinning.

"I knew it the moment you walked in," someone said.

"I don't hold in farts," said a bony Hispanic lying on his stomach. A public attorney walked by and two people in the cell asked if they would see the judge tonight. "It's ten now, they go until midnight on Saturday," said the public attorney. "You won't get called tonight, they'll start again at eight in the morning."

Around midnight a young Asian wearing many layers of clothing was put in the cell. He walked to the trashcan, leaned over it, took out four or five cheese sandwiches, and sat eating very quickly with unfocused eyes. Someone said "damn." Someone gave the young Asian their sandwich. A window-washer who punched someone in the subway said Central Booking in the Bronx had three floors you had to get through before you got to see a judge. "Be glad we aren't there," he said. "I've been there. When I was sixteen. People be in there three, four days before they see a judge." Around 2 a.m. breakfast was given. Sam ate his banana and small box of Frosted Flakes and gave someone his milk. He had a headache. He thought about calling Hester on the payphone. Hester didn't approve of shop-lifting. People started lying on the floor. Sam lay on the floor using his hoodie as a pillow.

"Damn, man, you stink," said the bony His-panic to the young Asian. "Get your stink-ass in the corner."

The bony Hispanic kicked the young Asian's back.

The young Asian moved in place with two jackets over his face.

"Don't move," said the bony Hispanic. "You're fanning your stink."

More people were put in the cell. There was no more room on the floor. Someone spilled their milk and three people stood. "Officer, I spilled my milk, can I get another," said the person loudly about five times.

Around 3 a.m. two inmates came into the cell to mop the floor.

"You missed a spot," said the bony Hispanic. "Come back, you missed a spot." The inmate with the mop stared at the bony Hispanic with a very angry facial expression. "You weak-ass inmate janitor," said the bony Hispanic. "You do a six-month stint at Riker's and you think you're hard. What did you do? Nine months? Six months for good behavior?" They screamed obscenities at each other. The inmate without a mop held back the inmate with the mop. The inmate with the mop had a facial expression like he was about to do something very out-of-control. Sam looked at a small Caucasian who had talked about stealing designer tuxedos and living under a bridge. The small Caucasian had a bored facial expression. The bony Hispanic was shouting obscenities at the inmate janitors who were now out of view. People were fanning the wet floor with their jackets. Sam lay in a near-fetal position with his hood around most of his face and thought about "Raweos." He woke around 6:30 a.m. to his name being called. He left the cell and walked past about six other cells. People in the other cells were sitting close together in small groups in front of giant fans. They stared at Sam with round eyes as Sam walked past. "They looked like lemurs," thought Sam standing with about fifty people in a wide hallway. Sam's name was called. He walked forward and stood in a line and the line moved upstairs into a large cell with about forty people inside. Around 10 a.m. Sam was called into a very small room where he sat opposite a public attorney. "You have no prior arrests, you'll get one day community service with a fine," said the public attorney through bars.

"I have a prior arrest," said Sam.

The public attorney stared at Sam.

"Don't say that," she said. "Don't tell me that."

"Oh," said Sam. "Okay. Thank you."

Sam went back to the large cell and sat staring at the window-washer who had punched someone in the subway. The window-washer was talking about different movies he had seen. "How long has he been talking," thought Sam. "Seems weird." Someone was talking about punching someone on an airplane to protect his children. About ten people were talking about drug deals. Someone was talking about how many years he would get and then threw his puffy jacket on the floor and smiled and said he was going to take a nap and lay stomach-down on the jacket. Around 12 p.m. Sam's named was called. He sat on a bench in a courtroom. He received one day of community service.

Outside the courthouse he called the organic vegan restaurant where he worked and said he would be an hour and a half late. He went to his apartment. He showered and emailed Robert. He drank two glasses of water. At work while putting on gloves he thought that he should have somehow asked for two days' community service so that his record could be erased again after six months.

"I thought you were calling because you wanted to go to Mara's party," said Robert the next night by Union Square. "I was sad."

"That's funny," said Sam. "You really wanted to go to her party."

"I was really looking forward to it," said Robert grinning.

Sam said he was having dinner with Hester

later and that he felt like it would be the last time he would see her because he felt like one of them would start uncontrollably talking a lot of shit about the other person. "I feel like that every time we see each other though," said Sam. "Then it's always okay for some reason."

"Do you like her," said Robert.

"Yeah," said Sam slowly. "I think I changed or something . . . like, I like being around someone who isn't like me a lot, in some ways, or something. I'm pretty sure I feel happy around her. I think I always feel good after I see her."

"What's wrong?" said Hester a few weeks later sitting on her bed facing Sam. "You're being quiet."

Sam lay holding a pillow, not looking at Hester.

"Nothing," he said in a quiet monotone.

"I can tell something's wrong. You just won't tell me. I can see it in your brains."

"Nothing," said Sam. "I'm just . . . have nothing to say."

"You're acting different," said Hester. "You're being like . . . pausing."

It was April and Hester's windows were open. They were on the fifth floor. Cars and voices could be heard from Twenty-Third Street. "I'm just sad or something," said Sam. "I feel normal. I'm just quiet."

"I feel kind of sad," said Hester. "I wish you would tell me your feelings sometimes."

"I don't have . . . anything to complain about," said Sam. "I'm just, I don't know, I don't want to talk anymore, I'll just start saying bad things." Sam covered his face with a blanket and rolled over on the bed. He stared at the blanket against his face. He lay without moving.

"You should say them," said Hester.

"I don't have anything to say. I'm not complaining."

"I'm not complaining either," said Hester. "I just wish we could be closer. I thought we could but I guess I was wrong." After a few minutes they began to say bad things about each other. Sam questioned Hester existentially while lying nearly facedown covered completely by the blanket. It was quiet and then Hester got off the bed.

"I'm going to sleep," she said. "So I can wake up tomorrow and live my 'goalless' life." Sam left the bedroom and saw Hester standing at her window looking outside. Sam left the apartment. In the staircase he text messaged Hester that he liked her, didn't have anything bad to say about her or her life, and didn't agree at all with anything he had said.

About a month later Robert and Sam were walking on St. Mark's Place around 10 p.m. Sam saw someone moving sideways like a crab on the street. Sam stopped walking and stared at the person. "Robert, wait," he said. "That person was in jail with me. He ate a lot of sandwiches really fast and someone kicked him. He didn't seem insane before."

Robert looked at Sam with an excited facial expression.

"He's wearing the exact same clothes, I think," said Sam.

The young Asian was about one hundred feet away.

"How is he walking so fast," said Sam in an expressive voice.

The young Asian stood on the corner of St. Mark's and Second Avenue repeatedly saying "Do you want to eat?" with unfocused eyes. The young Asian crossed the street and kicked over a metal trashcan.

"Do you think he really just wanted to eat?" said Robert.

"I don't know, that's funny," said Sam. "He ate a lot in jail."

Robert and Sam crossed the street and didn't

see the young Asian then saw him in the distance on a dark street. "He seems so fucked," said Sam. "He's moved around for like four blocks and no one seems to see him or something." Robert said the young Asian was probably a vampire. Sam said the young Asian talked to a public attorney in jail and sounded normal and said he lived with his girlfriend in the East Village. They followed the young Asian for about fifteen minutes. The young Asian was walking in different directions. Robert and Sam turned around sometimes. The young Asian noticed he was being followed. "I didn't rape my sister, two guys raped my sister, ask anyone, ask one of my friends," he said quietly to Sam.

A few weeks later around 1 a.m. Robert and Sam were on a bus to Atlantic City. Robert was reading a Bret Easton Ellis novel and Sam was reading printouts of the Wikipedia pages for Texas hold 'em and blackjack. Sam said he was going to eat a giant steak with A1 sauce if he won $2,000 or lost all but $20.

Around 5 a.m. at the Tropicana Sam was at a blackjack table and Robert was at a Texas hold 'em table. Sam text messaged Robert: "Up 400. Feel like impossible to lose. Want to leave soon?"

Robert text messaged: "Up 17. Coming in 20 minutes."

Around 6 a.m. on a down escalator Sam took a cell phone photo of $800 in hundreds and twenties and sent it to tips@gawker.com. Robert and Sam walked around looking for a buffet that was open. They took a cab to the other side of Atlantic City. They walked into the Borgata. About twenty minutes later Sam text messaged Robert: "Lost 600, steak soon. Excited."

Robert text messaged: "Lost 40, coming now."

"Hey," he said to Sam at the blackjack table.

"I'm just going to lose the rest really fast," said Sam grinning. "I'll save twenty dollars for steak." Three people Sam's age who didn't know each other were also at the blackjack table. After a few minutes Sam had $20 left. He and Robert walked around the casino smiling.

"I feel really good," said Sam. "How do you feel?"

"I feel really good also," said Robert.

"Should we go to the buffet," said Sam.

"I don't know," said Robert. "Do you want to?"

"I'm not sure. If we feel good we shouldn't eat at the buffet, right?"

Robert laughed. "Yeah, we probably shouldn't

eat at the buffet. I mean, I don't care, if you want to go I'll go." They got on a $2 trolley back to the Tropicana. It was around 9 a.m. and sunny. "What about that pizza place," said Sam pointing at a sign outside the trolley.

"I don't know, do you want to?" said Robert.

"No, not really. I'm not hungry, I think."

At the Tropicana they stood waiting for the bus to New York City.

"The Bodega is so far from the other casinos," said Sam.

"What do you mean," said Robert. "What bodega?"

"That place," said Sam. "With the sexy waitresses."

"The Borgata," said Robert.

"It should be called the Bodega," said Sam grinning. "That's funny, why would they name it something that sounds like 'bodega,' bodegas are like the shittiest stores that exist."

"Do you think you'll want to come back again?" said Robert.

"I don't know. I feel like I can't win. I would just lose all my money. But I feel happy here, I think."

"Do you want an avocado?" said Robert on the bus.

"No thank you," said Sam and closed his eyes.

At Penn Station Robert got on a train uptown to pet-sit. Sam went to his apartment and slept. The next night they were back in Atlantic City. They walked on the boardwalk by the beach around 4 a.m. "Everyone here seems, like, fucked, but in a good way," said Sam. "I feel at home here."

They walked into a deli and looked at shriveled potatoes.

"We should have a party here," said Robert on the street.

"We should just move here," said Sam.

"I feel like if I lived here I would just wake up every day and eat pizza, and play poker for two hours, and go home and watch TV, and drink beer," said Robert.

They walked past a strip bar and a house with a "For Rent" sign.

"I just want to be crying in someone's arms," said Robert.

A few months later Sam was sitting on his mattress with his MacBook drinking iced coffee and listening to music. It was around 3 p.m. and the room was very sunny. Sam had woken early that day and left his apartment and completed work in the library and came back to his apartment. "I want to do Pilates alone in my room to a DVD on my laptop every night," he said to Robert on Gmail chat. "I'm buying a Pilates mat once I'm unemployed. I'm creating a plan to be really good. So far I'm doing Pilates."

"That's great," said Robert.

"Are you serious," said Sam.

"Sort of," said Robert. "I mean, if I thought there was anything 'important' or something it would be being good." Robert said Sheila called twice earlier from the mental hospital and that he gave her Sam's phone number and told her to call Sam.

"Thanks," said Sam. "How is she."

"Sounded bad. The conversation started with her saying 'I think Sam brainwashed you. I like Sam. I like Stephen.' She just told me, like, things that didn't make sense. She said that drugs didn't have anything to do with her being there. That she put herself there."

"I wonder if she'll get better," said Sam.

"I felt sad. Connie was here. I felt funny about the situation. Later when Connie said things like 'why are you sad' I could say nothing and she would say things like 'are you worried about your friend.'"

"Haha," said Sam. "'Concrete reason.'"

"Yes," said Robert. "'Easy to understand.'"

They talked about Sheila for a few minutes.

"I thought about sex drive today," said Sam. "People with high motivation to have sex all the time don't like Lorrie Moore, I thought, citing Paul Mitchell and not really thinking more about it."

"That's funny," said Robert.

Sam said a person's name and said he wished their last name were "Lollapalooza." Robert said he also wished that. "I feel good that fast food exists even when I'm not eating it," said Robert. "I just think about it and feel better."

"I long for a Wendy's Spicy Chicken Sandwich," said Sam.

"We should get them together," said Robert.

"But I know I won't feel good eating it or after eating it," said Sam. "I only like thinking about it."

"We should buy them then throw them away," said Robert.

"Carry it around," said Sam. "I would do that."

It was getting dark out, or the sun had moved, and Sam's room was less bright. Sam looked around. His cup of iced coffee was empty. "I felt emotional today thinking about the past, like a year and a half ago, at Sheila's house," he said. "I think because I haven't been awake in the daytime for an extended period in so long and was reminded of the last time I was in a sunny room on a computer after having been up four to five hours, which was at Sheila's house, I think."

"Wow," said Robert.

"But there was nothing I could do with the emotion really," said Sam. "It just went away after a while."

About two months later it was November and Sam was at Joseph's house in Florida. Joseph had invited Sam to read at a "vegan brunch buffet" in a record store during a music festival. Joseph lived in a three-bedroom house with Chris where one bedroom was for Chris' record label. In the backyard were six tents and a school bus with a bunk bed and a sofa and no seats. Joseph gave Sam a pillow and a sleeping bag and said he could sleep on the bus the next two nights. They walked to a pizza place that also sold other things and bought iced coffee and pastries and sat outside on a street corner. It was around 2 p.m. "The weather is so nice here," said Sam. "Is that a Holiday Inn?"

"Yeah," said Joseph grinning. "I think it is."

Someone across the street was holding a sign promoting John McCain for president. "I like the people who hold the 9/11 conspiracy signs," said Joseph. "I think it's really funny."

"I would do that," said Sam.

"They just stand there the entire day holding a sign," said Joseph.

"We should get like twenty people to do it with us," said Sam.

They walked toward the University of Florida to see Chris' band Ghost Mice. Joseph said he stopped going to school when he was sixteen and saved money and left Kentucky on his bike without telling anyone and climbed onto a train, because he had heard of people doing that, and the train went somewhere but then came back and didn't move anymore and he bought a Greyhound ticket and went to San Francisco and then Arizona. After two months he called his father and said he was sorry and his father bought him a plane ticket and he went home and watched TV a lot and started to believe what he saw on TV was real. Sam asked Joseph if he became insane. "Yeah, I think so," said Joseph. "But I was the only one who knew, because I was alone all the time." Joseph said he then moved to Michigan and lived alone and became friends with Kaitlyn and then moved to Florida. Something flew toward Sam's face and Sam moved very fast.

"What was that," said Joseph laughing.

"An out-of-control butterfly," said Sam.

Joseph and Sam watched Ghost Mice and another band and then went back to Joseph's house and sat in Chris' room and listened to Joseph's band's new CD. Three people came into the room with five beers and sat on the floor. "I found myself lying on my back, looking up at nothing, in a hot dark room," sang Joseph on the CD. "In the middle of the day, today, I felt utterly confused." Joseph said he liked when the bass sounded like a whale. The CD ended and everyone went outside the house to go see a Japanese band at a bar. Someone said the bar wouldn't let them bring in beer.

"We can put them in our pockets," said Sam with his beer in his pocket.

"There's nowhere to put it on me," said a person in tight clothes and grinned.

They stood on the street drinking beer in the dark while looking at each other. Sam looked at the sky to see if there were a lot of stars. There seemed to be a normal amount of stars.

Around 11 p.m. Joseph and Sam left the bar and walked about thirty minutes to see Star Fucking Hipsters. At the venue Sam felt someone looking at him. Sam and the person stared at each other. Sam thought it might be a person named Audrey who he had talked to on the internet. Sam walked past the person and stood with Joseph facing the stage. "This is our attempt at a nonpolitical song, it's about how Jesus is a zombie," said the singer of Star Fucking Hipsters. "I mean, he is a zombie, he came from the dead. This song is saying it, that Jesus is actually a zombie. It's called 'Zombie Christ.'"

After the show the person and Sam stared at each other.

"Hi," said Sam.

"Hi," said the person.

"What's your name?" said Sam.

"Audrey, what's yours?"

Sam said his name and shook hands with Audrey and Audrey's friend Thomas. Joseph shook hands with Audrey. Sam looked at Joseph and heard Audrey say something to someone. Sam saw Audrey leaving. Sam and Joseph walked through the crowd toward the exit. They walked on the sidewalk toward Joseph's house. "I thought those people would hang out with us," said Sam. "We talked on the internet before and said we would hang out or something."

Around 2 a.m. Joseph ate toast with peanut butter while talking to Paul in the living room. Sam sat without talking. He had taken his contact lenses out and could not see people's facial expressions. More people came in the house. Joseph said he was going to sleep. Sam went in the kitchen and ate toast with olive oil. There was a bunk bed in the kitchen. People were laughing in the living room. Sam stared at things in the sink. He carried a piece of toast outside to the backyard. He went onto the bus and lay on the sofa in the dark.

He ate the toast and thought about being around people tomorrow. He thought about not talking while being around people. He thought about leaving without telling anyone. He thought about Joseph leaving on his bike without telling anyone. He zipped the sleeping bag shut around his body. People came on the bus using their cell phones for light. "Just so you know, I think there are roaches in here," said a girl.

"Oh, I'm not afraid of roaches," said a boy.

"Another person may be coming later," said the girl.

Sam text messaged Kaitlyn: "In Florida. I like Joseph."

The next morning outside the record store Sam saw Jeffrey and Sharon and Sharon's friends and introduced them to each other. Jeffrey said he drove 3 hours from Sarasota. He talked about his plan to roller-skate down four stories of the spiral-shaped structure inside the Guggenheim Museum to "break in" to the art world.

"That's really funny," said Sam. "Gawker would link probably."

"I ate a Sausage Egg McMuffin from McDonald's today," said Jeffrey.

There was a line of maybe thirty people for the "vegan brunch buffet."

Inside Sam stood with Jeffrey eating waffles, gravy, biscuits, tofu scramble, a cookie, a muffin, and other things. Sam said he wanted to get his stomach pumped after eating. Jeffrey said when he worked as a dishwasher in Alaska he was very bored and spent one shift imagining what it would be like if everything was made out of wood. Sam saw Audrey standing alone in line wearing all pink. Sam walked past Audrey to the bathroom. Sam walked out of the bathroom past Audrey without looking at her and talked to Jeffrey. Sharon drove Sam to a health-food store and Sam bought a "Synergy" brand kombucha. They drove back to the record store and Sam stood in front of people and said he was going to read from the beginning of his next book and then read about two people alone in rooms in Ohio and Pennsylvania talking to each other on

Gmail chat. Sam finished and sat by Jeffrey and said he felt like a little bitch.

"I don't feel that you're a little bitch," said Jeffrey.

"I mean, I feel okay, or something," said Sam.

"Oh, this is my friend Gina," said Jeffrey.

Sam smiled at Gina and said "hi."

"Inspirational," said Audrey in a loud monotone looking down at Sam.

"Good," said Sam. "You came. I'm glad you came."

A man in an orange shirt said Sam was "the shit."

Someone asked Sam to sign a book. Sam drew a toy poodle and wrote "666" on its forehead. Sam didn't see Audrey then saw her standing to the left. Sharon asked Sam if he still wanted to eat dinner with her and other University of Florida MFA students. Sam said he did and that one of them would call the other one. Sam stood and said "Do you want to go to American Apparel?" to Audrey with three or four people looking at him.

"Sure," said Audrey with a serious facial expression.

Someone said something to Sam about Columbus, Ohio. Sam thanked the person and walked to Joseph and said he was going to hang out with his friend from Sarasota.

Jeffrey, Gina, Audrey, and Sam walked toward Jeffrey's car. Sam said he saw Star Fucking Hipsters in Brooklyn a week ago and the singer wasn't drunk at all then four or five songs later was extremely drunk and swung his guitar at the audience and the audience stared at him. Jeffrey and Audrey talked to each other. Sam looked at Gina not talking to anyone. Audrey sat in the front seat of Jeffrey's car. At American Apparel Sam bought blue organic underwear. Outside he held the underwear to his face and said "sustainable." They walked on the sidewalk and Audrey and Sam talked about "the death-metal voice." Sam told Audrey to scream "red shirt" at people across the street walking in the same direction as them.

"Red shirt," screamed Audrey.

A woman in her forties, two teenagers, and a person in a bright red shirt who was maybe twenty turned their upper bodies and looked at Audrey while walking forward. "It's a family, I think," said Sam. "They're ignoring it. That's so bad for them, a family, it'll probably be all they talk about later, like when they're eating."

Sam walked forward for a few seconds without thinking anything.

"They're right there," he said laughing. "We're like right next to them."

"That's why we need to slow down," said Audrey grinning a little.

They walked around Gainesville for about thirty minutes.

"We should go to the beach," said Sam.

"I would go to the beach," said Jeffrey. "Do you want to?"

Sam said he didn't have swimming shorts. He said he wanted to sit in a park and lie on the grass and drink iced coffee and maybe beer while relaxing in sunlight. Jeffrey said he would do that. Sam pulled a sign out of the ground that said "Yes on 4" and had a drawing of a bear. "We should put it in the ground by where we sit," said Sam and put it in Jeffrey's car.

They bought iced coffee and drove to the University of Florida campus and walked around. "The grass looks dead in this area," said Sam holding his MacBook. "There is no life in this area." He pointed at people sitting on the grass throwing food in each other's mouths. Audrey said something about Jesus. Sam said it was a club for throwing food in each other's mouths. Sam said he felt jealous. Jeffrey was holding the "Yes on 4" sign and a half-gallon Odwalla green juice about one-third full.

"You really look like a hardcore activist," said Sam laughing.

"Why should we vote yes on 4," said a middle-aged woman sitting on a lawn chair in a large group of people about thirty feet away.

"I don't know," said Jeffrey not looking at the woman.

"No, tell us why we should vote yes on 4," said the middle-aged woman.

"I don't know why," said Jeffrey. "I'm just carrying the sign."

"Here, you can have it, do you want it," said Jeffrey in a quiet voice.

"No, don't," said Sam. "We need it to put by where we sit."

They sat on a large area of grass by a crocodile monument and Sam put the "Yes on 4" sign in the ground and opened his MacBook. There was no internet access without a password. It was sunny and maybe 70 degrees. Sam lay on his back. Jeffrey lay on his stomach. Audrey lay on her back.

"Where is Gina," said Sam.

"She went to take photographs," said Jeffrey.

Sam asked Audrey about the band she was seeing tonight.

Audrey said Sam should go with her to see the band.

"Everybody always said that Krispy Kreme was supposed to be so delicious but then I tasted one and I said 'what's so special about these?'" said Jeffrey with a bored facial expression. Sam laughed and said "That would be a good commercial for Dunkin' Donuts" and recorded Jeffrey repeating what he had said into his MacBook.

"When did you eat the Sausage Egg McMuffin," said Sam.

"This morning," said Jeffrey. "Before we left."

Sam saw Jeffrey drinking from his half-gallon of Odwalla and laughed.

"Stop laughing at my Odwalla," said Jeffrey grinning.

"Can I see it?" said Sam. "It's really funny."

Sam threw the half-gallon container very far away.

"Go get it," said Jeffrey.

"Are you angry I threw your Odwalla," said Sam.

"Not really," said Jeffrey.

Sam said he would roll like a log to go get it. But he was facing the wrong direction. "Roll to go get it, Audrey," he said. "You're facing the right direction."

Audrey started rolling. Sam saw that Jeffrey looked bored.

"It's funny you got her to do that," said Jeffrey.

"You're rolling wrong," said Sam. "You're turning."

"No, wait," said Audrey rolling on the grass.

"Now you need to roll, like, vertically," said Sam.

Audrey held the Odwalla and stood. The Odwalla fell in an ant pile. "Ant pile," said Sam. Audrey threw the Odwalla. Sam picked up the Odwalla and they stood in a triangle throwing the Odwalla at each other. "Jeffrey, you're not throwing it like a football," said Sam. "Throw it overhand like a football." The container of Odwalla broke on the grass. "Are you okay," said Sam grinning at Jeffrey. "I'll buy you another one." Gina put the broken Odwalla container in a trashcan. Sam pointed at something on the grass and said "Jump over that" to Audrey. "Jump over what," said Audrey. "The bush thing," said Sam. "Plant. Or fern, perhaps." Audrey ran and jumped over the side of the plant. "You didn't jump over it at all," said Sam. "You just jumped over air." Sam ran and jumped over the middle of the plant. Audrey ran and jumped over the side of the plant. Sam jumped over it again then stood staring at different things. Gina said she took a photo of an old man holding a can of Dr Pepper in each hand while staring at a squirrel. Sam walked around a little then saw Audrey sitting on a bench looking at him with vines above her head. Sam smiled and put his hands in his pockets and looked at the ground. "What are we going to do," he said. "I mean, I don't know, we're in a park right now, I feel good right now, I feel like I'll just kill myself after this."

Jeffrey, Gina, and Audrey were looking at Sam.

"We're in a park, or something," said Sam grinning.

"Don't kill yourself," said Jeffrey.

"I don't know what to do," said Sam.

"People expect you to kill yourself now," said Jeffrey.

"Really?" said Sam. "I don't know. Maybe an asteroid will hit me after my next two books come out. I don't know. I honestly don't know what to do, like, overall, or something."

"Draw hamsters," said Audrey.

"I already did that," said Sam.

"There's nothing left for you," said Audrey.

Sam walked around then kicked his foot making his shoe go very far away. He ran to his shoe and put it back on. He stood on the grass without looking at anything specific.

"Your shoes are ugly," said Audrey.

"My shoes, no," said Sam looking at his shoes.

Audrey stepped on Sam's shoe. "Now it's okay," she said. "I'll do the other one." She stepped on the other shoe. "That feels good," said Sam staring at his shoes trying to think about something. He wasn't really thinking anything, he thought.

Near Jeffrey's car Audrey got on a bike locked to a bike rack and tried to pedal. Jeffrey and Gina walked ahead. Audrey looked at Sam while trying to pedal. "Try pedaling harder," said Sam.

At Jeffrey's car Sam asked Audrey if he could sit in front.

"Sure," said Audrey. "Why are you asking me? It's not my car."

"I don't know," said Sam. "You were sitting in front before."

"Yes, you can sit in front," said Audrey.

Sam sat in the front seat and said "yes" in an expressive voice while moving his fist in the air and staring at Jeffrey. "Do you do that," said

Sam. "Do you 'pump your fist' ever?" Jeffrey said sometimes he did. Audrey pushed a wooden sword into the front seat and Sam held the blade and pushed it so the handle went against Audrey's chest. At a stoplight Sam screamed "Obama" at someone watering grass with a hose. They parked and went in a Vietnamese restaurant. Audrey ordered "the Princess Bowl." Jeffrey ordered "the Chicken Noodle Bowl." They finished eating and sat on a street corner looking at people across the street playing instruments and asking people for money. Audrey pointed at a feature of Sam's shoes and said she didn't notice that when she said Sam's shoes were ugly.

"Are they like pirates," said Jeffrey about the people across the street.

"I think they are," said Sam. "Pirates heckle."

Jeffrey looked at Sam and said he was going back to Sarasota.

"Do you need a ride to your car?" he said to Audrey near his car.

"I'm parked just over there," said Audrey.

Sam stood with Jeffrey on the driver's side.

Jeffrey gave Sam some of his drawings.

"Thank you for coming," said Sam. "I liked hanging out with you."

"Me too," said Jeffrey and then said a long sentence Sam responded to by making noises and nodding while thinking about how Audrey and Gina were standing in view, near the other side of the car, without talking to each other or looking at anyone.

"Do you want a ride to your car?" said Jeffrey to Audrey.

"No, I'm parked just over there," said Audrey.

"Weird," thought Sam. "He already asked that."

Jeffrey and Gina got in the car. Sam saw Audrey walking away. "Wait, where are you going," he said. "I'm alone." Audrey walked toward Sam with a self-conscious facial expression. "We've pretty much done everything we can in Gainesville," she said quickly. "Yup, there's nothing left to do in Gainesville. We've done everything."

"What are we going to do," said Sam.

"We can follow someone," said Audrey.

They followed a small group of people in a band that Sam liked for about ten blocks. Someone offered Audrey twenty cents for a cigarette. Audrey said she didn't have one. The person gave Audrey twenty cents. Audrey offered someone twenty cents for a cigarette. The person didn't have one. "You should have screamed 'fuck' when he didn't have one," said Sam and turned and saw Audrey trying to open a locked door.

"Fuck," she screamed with a serious facial expression.

Sam laughed. "Good job," he said. "I want iced tea."

They sat on a curb with iced tea and a double espresso. It was getting dark out. American Apparel was in view. Someone on the street messed up a trick on their skateboard. "You can't skate," shouted Audrey.

"What," said the person skating away.

Audrey shouted "Obama" at the person.

"That was good," said Sam. "You dominated him a lot."

"I have an idea or something," said Sam. "We should start from very far away and then run toward each other and then give each other high fives jumping in the air."

"Let's do it," said Audrey beginning to stand.

"No, wait," said Sam. "It's better just to think about it."

Audrey said something agreeing with Sam.

"Now what," said Sam.

"I don't know," said Audrey.

It was quiet outside.

People were walking around.

Sam thought about what he was going to say.

"Do you want to go to that show at UF?" he said.

"Yes," said Audrey.

On the University of Florida campus they went into the building the concert hall was in and each went in a bathroom. Sam came out and saw a missed call from Sharon. He text messaged Sharon that he would not be going to dinner. He walked around and didn't see Audrey. There were many college students in the building. About twenty minutes later Sam saw Audrey walking out of the concert hall. They walked into the concert hall and sat against the back wall for about an hour. Audrey said one time she found a half-eaten watermelon inside a giant bush. They left the building around 9 p.m. and sat or stood in different places on campus. They walked into a very dark area with a small lake and a forest.

"Oh, this is where Ghost Mice played yesterday," said Sam.

"I was here," said Audrey. "Thomas saw you. He was like 'there's Sam.' I was like 'oh.' I didn't see you."

"I didn't know you were here," said Sam.

Audrey said there was a path around the lake.

She walked ahead of Sam into the forest. "This is good," said Sam and saw car lights. "Wait, there's a road right there. The road is ruining it for us." Audrey laughed a little and held a palm frond out of the path. Sam walked past her and saw a chair and quickly sat on it. Audrey looked at Sam sitting on the chair. Sam stood and moved the chair onto the path. Audrey sat on the chair facing the lake. Sam stood behind her and massaged her head and she said it felt good. Her eyes were closed and she made quiet noises sometimes. Sam felt her leaning backwards into him. He looked at the moonlight reflected off the lake. He looked down and felt that he had seen Audrey at the end of a motion where she had looked up at him furtively. Sam thought about leaning down and kissing her while still standing behind her, with his head sideways, or upside-down a little, or something. Sam looked at the lake. He looked at Audrey's nose ring. He leaned over and kissed her mouth and moved to the front of the chair while kissing her and she stood and they kissed for about ten minutes. "Do you want to go back to my car?" she said. "Yes," said Sam. They kissed some more then stared at each other with neutral facial expressions. Sam thought that her facial expression was as neutral as Sheila's when

Sheila was in similar situations. Sam felt his own neutral facial expression. They walked out of the forest. People asked for their wristbands to get into the concert. They took off their wristbands and gave them to the people.

"Now what," said Audrey in her car.

"Are you hungry?" said Sam.

"Not really. Are you?"

"I don't know," said Sam. "No, not really."

They drove without talking for about ten minutes. A Rilo Kiley song played on repeat. Outside people were walking around or standing in groups on sidewalks. "We could go there," said Sam about a shopping plaza. "Never mind, there isn't anything there. I thought there was a Publix."

"Where does Chris live?" said Audrey in a voice louder than normal.

They parked near Chris' house and Sam opened his car door. "You're leaving?" said Audrey. "That's it? Well, okay, bye."

Sam stared at Audrey with his hand on the door handle.

"That's it," she said. "We're not going to hang out? Alright."

"Do you want to come in?" said Sam.

"Yes. I thought you were leaving."

"I thought you were coming with me," said Sam.

"Me too," said Audrey. "Sorry, maybe I mumbled."

"I'm afraid of going in the house," said Sam near the house. "When I'm inside they just stare at me and I don't say anything. I'm going to call the one person I know."

Sam called Joseph. There was no answer.

Audrey said she didn't want to go in the house.

"Everyone will be like 'who's this girl,'" she said.

They opened a wooden gate and walked into the backyard. They saw people through a window moving around and laughing inside the house. They walked by the school bus and sat side-by-side at a picnic table. It was dark and quiet in the backyard. Sam took out his MacBook and asked Audrey if she wanted to check her email. "I don't check my email," she said. "My Toshiba broke. I don't even have Gmail." Sam started playing a song on his MacBook and said he liked the song and stopped it at eight seconds. Audrey said something about the drums being good. Sam put his MacBook in his backpack. They sat looking ahead, away from the house, at some tents and a fence and another house. Sam felt Audrey touching his head a little.

"I can't do the massage thing," she said quietly and stopped touching him.

There was a thing on the table and Sam touched it.

"What is this," he said.

They touched the thing and looked at it.

"So you're going back tomorrow?" said Audrey.

"Yeah," said Sam. "My plane is at seven."

"Am I ever going to see you again?"

"I don't know," said Sam after a few seconds.

"I want to go to New York City," said Audrey.

"When?" said Sam.

"Soon," said Audrey.

"What would you go for?"

"A better life," said Audrey.

"Oh, you want to move there." Sam looked at his cell phone and opened and closed it a few times. He laid his head on his arms facing away from Audrey. People in the house were talking and playing acoustic guitar.

"Well, I'll probably just head back soon," said Audrey.

"Okay," said Sam and put his elbows on the table. "A mosquito bit my face last night," he said. "When I was sleeping on the bus." He touched his cheek and turned toward Audrey. He looked at her face as she looked at his cheek. He looked down at his cell phone in his lap.

"My cell phone is almost out of batteries," he said.

"That sucks. You'll probably need it tomorrow."

They sat quietly for about ten seconds. There were faraway sounds of people doing things in other parts of the town.

"What did you want to be when you grew up?" said Audrey.

"Marine biologist," said Sam.

TITLES IN THE COMPANION SERIES
THE ART OF THE NOVELLA

BARTLEBY THE SCRIVENER / HERMAN MELVILLE

THE LESSON OF THE MASTER / HENRY JAMES

MY LIFE / ANTON CHEKHOV

THE DEVIL / LEO TOLSTOY

THE TOUCHSTONE / EDITH WHARTON

THE HOUND OF THE BASKERVILLES / ARTHUR CONAN DOYLE

THE DEAD / JAMES JOYCE

FIRST LOVE / IVAN TURGENEV

A SIMPLE HEART / GUSTAVE FLAUBERT

THE MAN WHO WOULD BE KING / RUDYARD KIPLING

MICHAEL KOHLHAAS / HEINRICH VON KLEIST

THE BEACH OF FALESÁ / ROBERT LOUIS STEVENSON

THE HORLA / GUY DE MAUPASSANT

THE ETERNAL HUSBAND / FYODOR DOSTOEVSKY

THE MAN THAT CORRUPTED HADLEYBURG / MARK TWAIN

THE LIFTED VEIL / GEORGE ELIOT

THE GIRL WITH THE GOLDEN EYES / HONORÉ DE BALZAC

A SLEEP AND A FORGETTING / WILLIAM DEAN HOWELLS

BENITO CERENO / HERMAN MELVILLE

MATHILDA / MARY SHELLEY

STEMPENYU: A JEWISH ROMANCE / SHOLEM ALEICHEM

FREYA OF THE SEVEN ISLES / JOSEPH CONRAD

HOW THE TWO IVANS QUARRELLED / NIKOLAI GOGOL

MAY DAY / F. SCOTT FITZGERALD

RASSELAS, PRINCE ABYSSINIA / SAMUEL JOHNSON

THE DECEITFUL MARRIAGE / MIGUEL DE CERVANTES

THE LEMOINE AFFAIR / MARCEL PROUST

THE COXON FUND / HENRY JAMES

THE DEATH OF IVAN ILYICH / LEO TOLSTOY

TALES OF BELKIN / ALEXANDER PUSHKIN

OTHER TITLES IN
THE CONTEMPORARY ART OF THE NOVELLA SERIES

THE PATHSEEKER / IMRE KERTÉSZ
THE DEATH OF THE AUTHOR / GILBERT ADAIR
THE NORTH OF GOD / STEVE STERN
CUSTOMER SERVICE / BENOÎT DUTEURTRE
BONSAI / ALEJANDRO ZAMBRA
ILLUSION OF RETURN / SAMIR EL-YOUSSEF
CLOSE TO JEDENEW / KEVIN VENNEMANN
A HAPPY MAN / HANSJÖRG SCHERTENLEIB
SHOPLIFTING FROM AMERICAN APPAREL / TAO LIN
LUCINELLA / LORE SEGAL
SANDOKAN / NANNI BALESTRINI